For the Henleys, the Lewises, and Nana
C. H.

For Rosalind, Emily, & Julia Stevenson
F. K.

Text and illustrations © 1993 by Claire Henley. All rights reserved. Printed in Italy. First published 1993 by J. M. Dent & Sons, Ltd., Orion House, 5 Upper St. Martin's Lane, London, WC2H 9EA, England. First published in the United States of America by Hyperion Books for Children, 114 Fifth Avenue, New York, New York 10011.

FIRST EDITION

1 3 5 7 9 10 8 6 4 2

Library of Congress Catalog Card Number: 92–72024
ISBN: 1–56282–340–X/1–56282–341–8 (lib. bdg.)

Sunny Day

Claire Henley

Hyperion Books for Children
New York

It's sunny today.
The sky is clear and blue.
There is not a single cloud in sight.

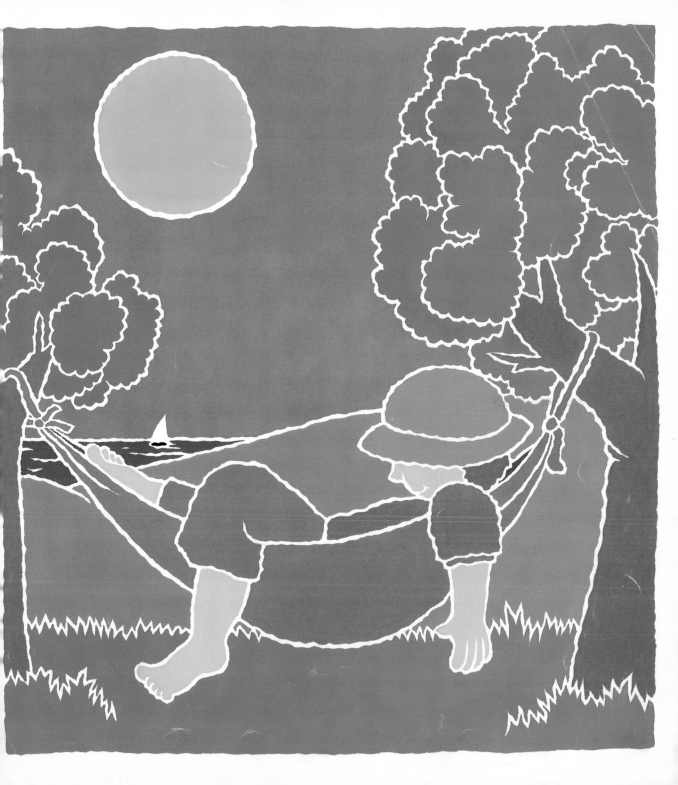

In the garden striped bees buzz and hum.
Butterflies dance in the warm breeze.

Brightly colored flowers open their petals
and turn their heads toward the sun.
It is hot and still.

A spotted lizard basks on the wall.
Its eyes blink. Its tongue flicks in and out.
Two fat black beetles crawl slowly
into the shade.

It's a perfect day for a picnic.
We can walk down to the beach.
Look! The tide is in.

We need swimsuits and towels,
buckets and spades.
Let's go! Come on, Timmy,
we'll take you, too!

A sleepy cat stretches and purrs.
It feels lazy.
It lies down under the cool green
leaves for a long sleep.

High above, we watch swallows darting
to and fro above the rooftops.

The sun feels hot on our heads.
It's a good thing we've brought our hats.
The sand burns our bare toes.

There's the sea. Let's race!
We run and splash in the cold waves.

Time for ice cream.
It melts and makes our fingers sticky –
but we don't mind.

The sun goes down.
It's getting cooler.
Sunny days are lots of fun.